DEMON GUN

CHAPTER 1
To Whom Vengeance Belongs

Demon Gun
was created by

Gary Cohn, writer
Barry Orkin, penciller, additional inks
Peter Palmiotti, inker
Kurt Hathaway, letterer
Steven Chin, editor

GRAND DESIGN
PUBLISHING

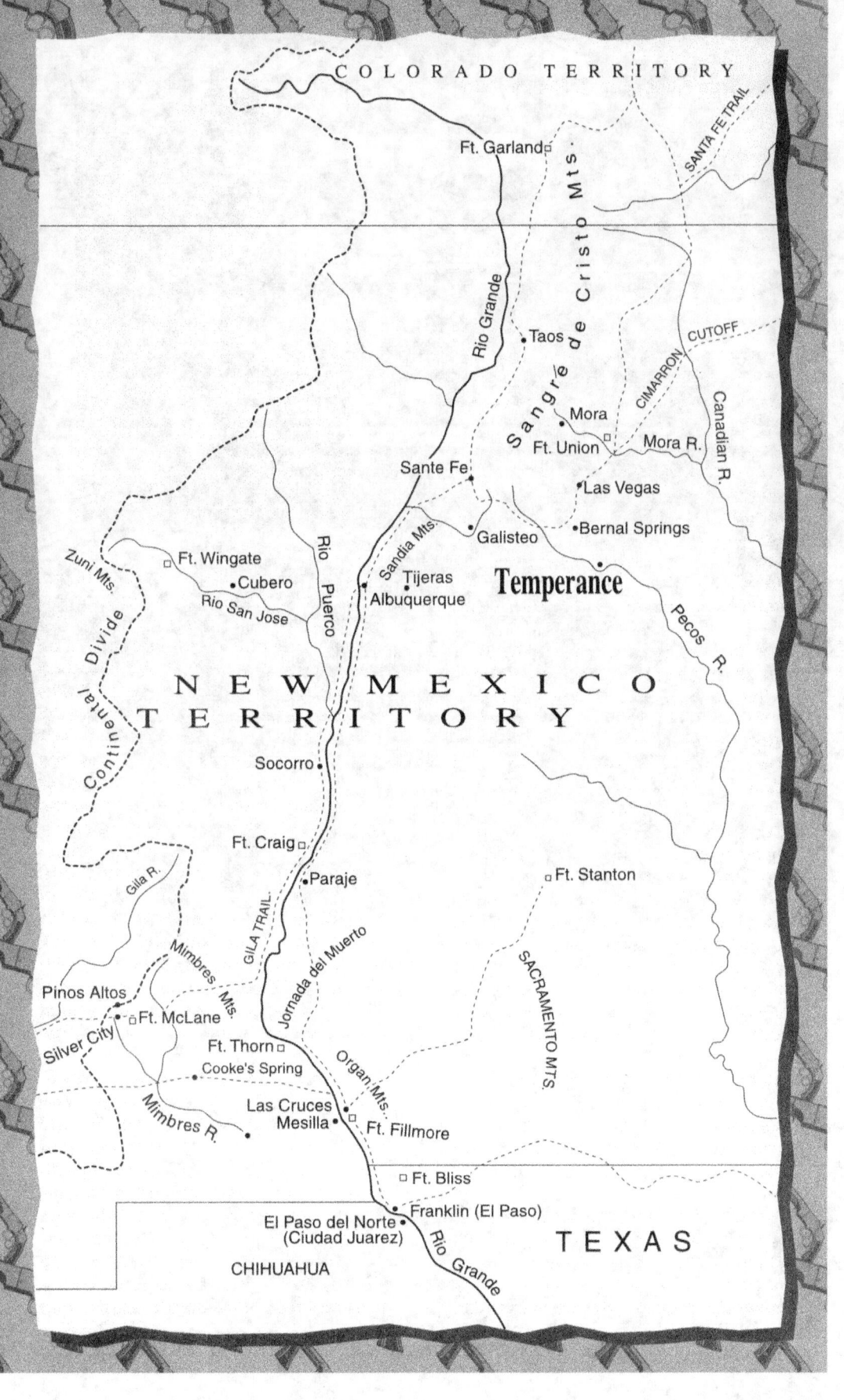

Demon Gun ™

Psalm 94

O Lord God, to whom vengeance belongeth,
O God, to whom vengeance belongeth, shew Thyself.
Lift up Thyself, Thou proud judge of the earth: render a reward to the proud.
Lord, how long shall the wicked, how long shall the wicked triumph?
How long shall they utter and speak hard things?
and all the workers of iniquity boast themselves?
They break in pieces Thy people, O Lord, and afflict Thine heritage.
They slay the widow and the stranger, and murder the fatherless.
Yet they say, The Lord shall not see, neither shall the God of Jacob regard it.
Understand, ye brutish among the people, and ye fools, when will ye be wise?
He that planted the ear, shall He not hear?
He that formed the eye, shall He not see?
He that chastiseth the heathen, shall He not correct?
He that teacheth man knowledge, shall He not know?
The Lord knoweth the thoughts of man, that they are vanity.
Blessed is the man whom Thou chastenest, O Lord,
and teachest him out Thy Law;
That Thou mayest give him rest from the days of adversity,
until the pit be digged for the wicked.
For the Lord will not cast off his people,
neither will he forsake his inheritance.
But judgement shall return unto righteousness:
and all the upright in heart shall follow it.
Who will rise up for me against evildoers?
or who will stand up for me against the workers of iniquity?
Unless The Lord had been my help, my soul had almost dwelt in silence.
When I said, my foot slippeth: Thy mercy, O Lord, held me up.
In the multitude of my thoughts within me Thy comforts delight my soul.
Shall the throne of iniquity have fellowship with Thee,
which frameth mischief by a Law?
They gather themselves together against the soul of the righteous,
and condemn the innocent blood.
But The Lord is my defence: and my God is the rock of my refuge.
And He shall bring upon them their own iniquity,
and shall cut them off in their wickedness:

yea, The Lord our God shall cut them off.

CRUSADE

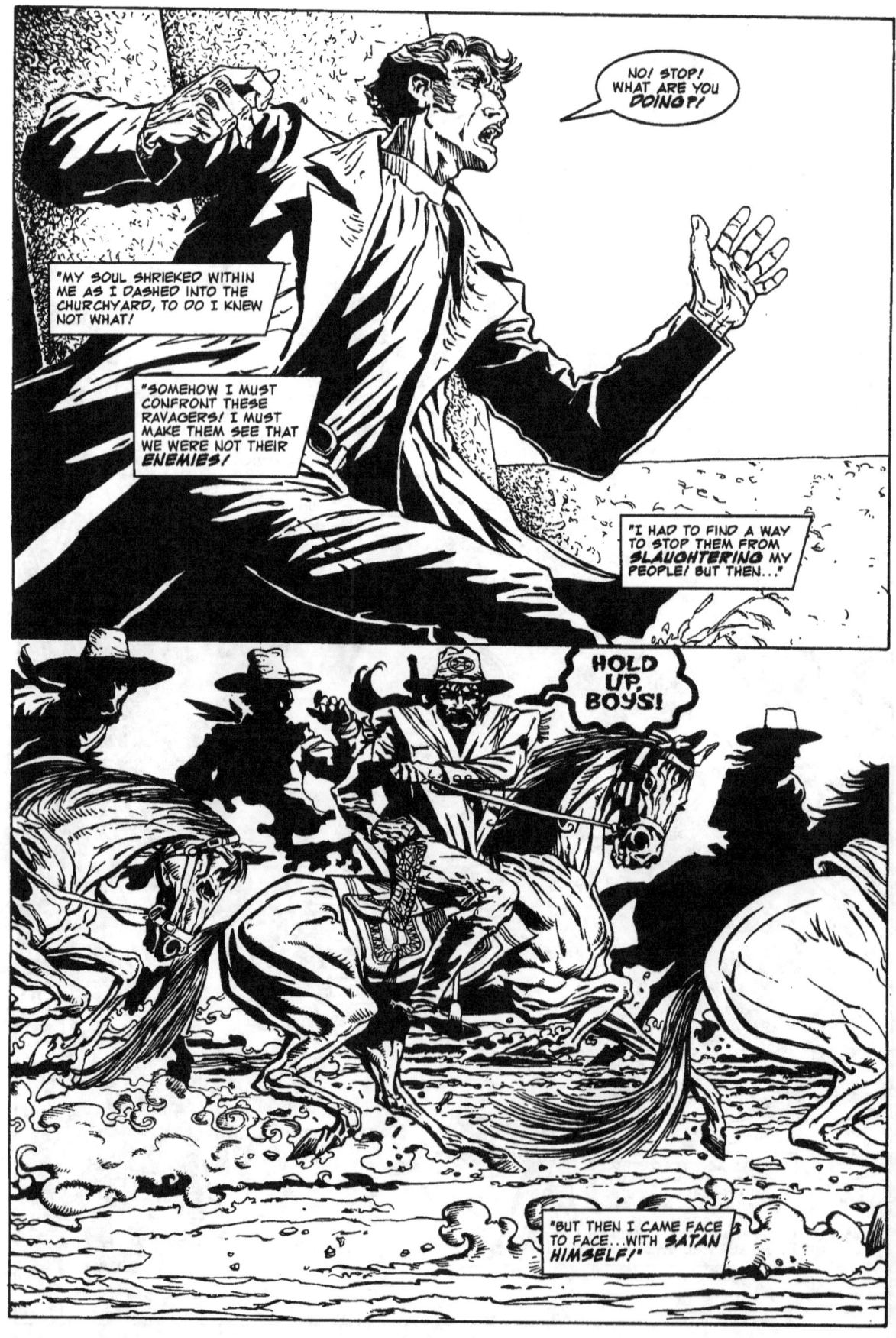

CHAPTER 2
Oh Lord, Thou Hast Searched Me

Demon GUN™

Psalm 139

O Lord, thou hast searched me, and known me.

Thou knowest my downsitting and mine uprising, thou understandest my thought afar off.

Thou compassest my path and my lying down, and art acquainted with all my ways.

For there is not a word in my tongue, but, lo, O Lord, thou knowest it altogether.

Thou hast beset me behind and before, and laid thine hand upon me.

Such knowledge is too wonderful for me; it is high, I cannot attain to it.

Whither shall I go from thy spirit? or wither shall I flee from thy presence?

If I ascend up into heaven, thou art there: if I make my bed in hell, behold, thou art there.

If I take the wings of the morning, and dwell in the uttermost parts of the sea:

Even there shall thy hand lead me, and thy right hand shall hold me.

If I say, Surely the darkness shall cover me; even the night shall be light about me.

Yea, the darkness hideth not from thee; but the night shineth as the day:

the darkness and the light are both alike to thee.

For thou hast possessed my reins: thou hast covermd me in my mother's womb.

I will praise thee; for I am fearfully and wonderfully made:

marvellous are thy works; and that my soul knoweth right well.

My substance was not hid from thee, when I was made in secret,

and curiously wrought in the lowest parts of the earth.

Thine eyes did see my substance, yet being unperfect;

and in thy book all my members were written,

which in continuance were fashioned, when as yet there was none of them.

How precious also are thy thoughts unto me O God! how great is the sum of them!

If I should count them, they are more in number than the sand:

when I awake, I am still with thee.

Surely thou wilt slay the wicked, O God; depart from me, therefore, ye bloody men.

For they speak against thee wickedly, and thine enemies take thy name in vain.

Do not I hate them, O Lord, that hate thee?

and am not I grieved with those that rise up against thee?

I hate them with perfect hatred: I count them mine enemies.

Search me, O God, and know my heart: try me, and know my thoughts:

And see if there be any wicked way in me,

and lead me in the way everlasting.

Also out of the midst thereof came the likeness of living creatures. And this was their appearance; they had the likeness of a man.

And they went every one straight forward: whither the spirit was to go, they went; and they turned not when they went.

As for the likeness of the living creature, their appearance was like burning coals of fire...

MARIA...! UNH....!

Thou art all fair, my love; there is no spot in thee.

Thou hast ravished my heart with one of thine eyes, with one chain of thy neck.

HARLOT! WHORE! HOW DARE YOU?!

CLOTHE THY NAKEDNESS, HARLOT!

For the commandment is a lamp, and the law is light; to keep thee from the evil woman, from the flattery of the tongue of a strange woman!

Lust not after her beauty in thine heart! Neither let her take thee with her eyelids.

BUT... I...I LOVE YOU...

BLASPHEMY! I GIVE YOU PURITY...

...YOU OFFER ME OFFAL!

PLEASE...

I KNOW YOU NOW FOR A TOOL OF THE DEVIL.

YOU ARE LOATHESOME. I WILL NO LONGER TOLERATE THE SIGHT OF YOU.

CHAPTER 3

Oh Lord, Rebuke Me Not...

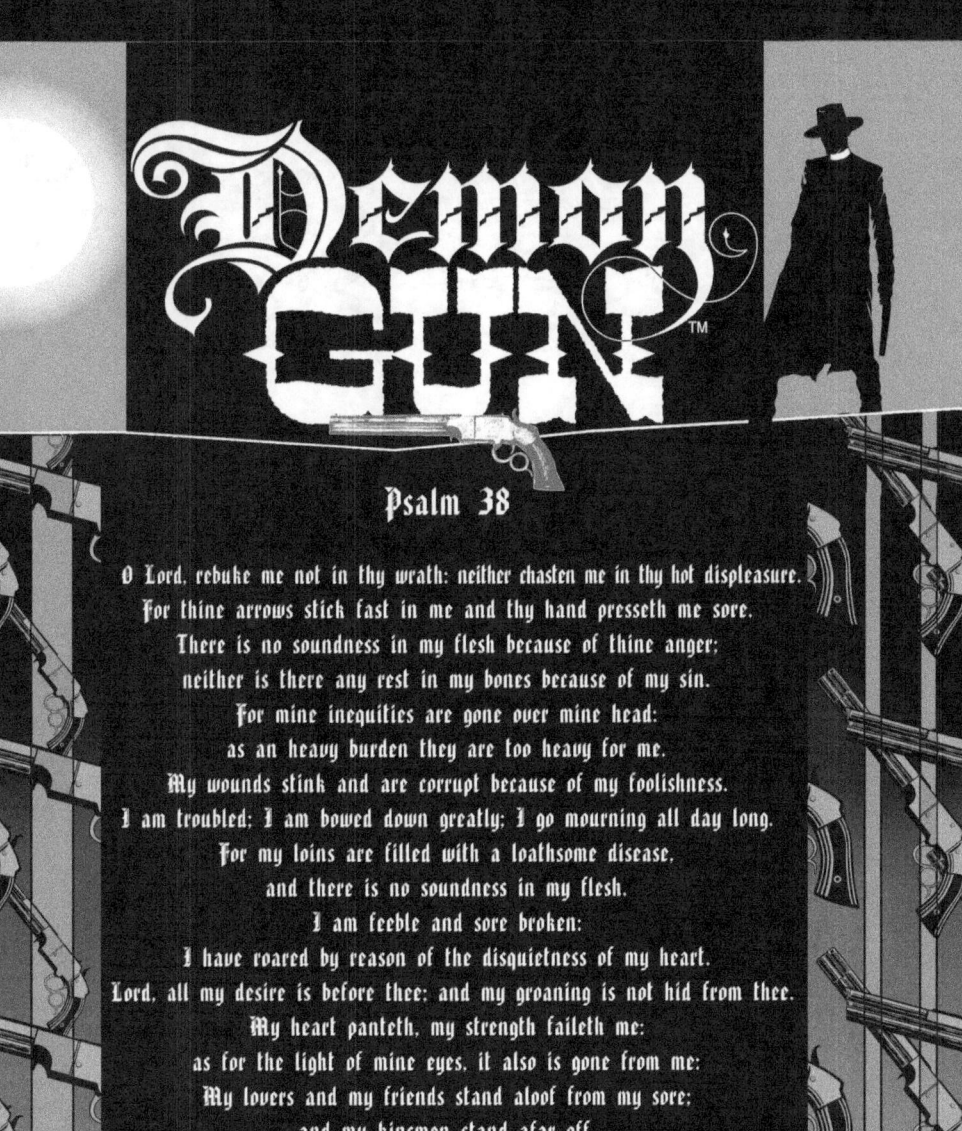

Demon GUN™

Psalm 38

O Lord, rebuke me not in thy wrath: neither chasten me in thy hot displeasure.

For thine arrows stick fast in me and thy hand presseth me sore.

There is no soundness in my flesh because of thine anger;

neither is there any rest in my bones because of my sin.

For mine iniquities are gone over mine head:

as an heavy burden they are too heavy for me.

My wounds stink and are corrupt because of my foolishness.

I am troubled; I am bowed down greatly; I go mourning all day long.

For my loins are filled with a loathsome disease,

and there is no soundness in my flesh.

I am feeble and sore broken:

I have roared by reason of the disquietness of my heart.

Lord, all my desire is before thee: and my groaning is not hid from thee.

My heart panteth, my strength faileth me:

as for the light of mine eyes, it also is gone from me;

My lovers and my friends stand aloof from my sore;

and my kinsmen stand afar off.

They also that seek after my life lay snares for me:

and they that seek my hurt speak mischievous things,

and imagine deceits all the day long.

But I, as a deaf man, heard not:

and I was as a dumb man that openeth not his mouth.

Thus I was as a man that heareth not,

and in whose mouth are no reproofs.

For in thee, O Lord, do I hope: thou wilt hear, O Lord my God.

For I said, Hear me, lest otherwise they should rejoice over me:

when my foot slippeth, they magnify themselves against me.

For I am ready to halt, and my sorrow is continually before me.

For I will declare mine iniquity; I will be sorry for my sin.

But mine enemies are lively, and they are strong:

and they that hate me wrongfully are multiplied.

They also that render evil for good are mine adversaries;

because I follow the thing that good is.

Forsake me not, O Lord: O my God, be not far from me.

Make haste to help me, O Lord my salvation.

YOU WOULD HAVE BEEN *WISE* TO LISTEN TO COLONEL QUAIL, MAJOR.

SNIKT

BUT THEN, YOU COULDN'T RESIST THE PROMISE OF MY CARESS!

NEXT TIME DON'T COME TO A WOMAN'S BED WITH A KNIFE IN YOUR BOOT!

OF COURSE...FOR YOU THERE WILL NOT BE A *NEXT* TIME!

I KNEW YOU WOULDN'T LET ME DOWN, MARIA!

HE'S OUT THERE SOMEWHERE-- THE PREACHER!

AND YOU'RE GONNA LEAD ME RIGHT TO HIM!

I THOUGHT ME AN' PREACHER HOWE HAD SAID ALL WE HAD TO SAY WHEN I GUTSHOT HIM AND BURNED HIS CHURCH DOWN AROUND HIM.

BUT IT SEEMS HE'S BEEN HUNTIN' ME EVER SINCE, AND WE'VE GOT TO HAVE US ONE MORE CONVERSATION IF MY PLAN IS GONNA SUCCEED!

AND YOU, MARIA, ARE THE KEY TO HOWE...

LEASTWISE, THAT'S WHAT MY *DOG* TELLS ME!

IN THAT TIME OUR TWO COMMUNITIES GREW CLOSE.

PERHAPS IRON SHIRT'S SCOUTS KNEW WE WERE THERE. PERHAPS WE WERE MERELY FORTUNATE. BUT FOR LONG WEEKS WE WERE UNMOLESTED.

MEANWHILE MY PEOPLE TORE APART OUR WAGONS AND USED THE WOOD TO BUILD A DEFENSIVE *PALISADE* AND BUILDINGS.

WE EVEN BEGAN WORK ON A *PROPER* CHURCH.

BUT ALTHOUGH PADRE UMBERTO BEAMED AT US, I KEPT OUR PEOPLE AS SEPARATE AS POSSIBLE.

AFTER ALL, DESPITE THEIR APPARENT GOODNESS, THE PEOPLE OF LA PLACIDA WERE INDIOS, AND *PAPISTS!*

THE COMANCHES WERE NOT THE *ONLY ONES* OUR WALL WAS INTENDED TO KEEP AT BAY.

A--ANGEL OF THE LORD...?
ANGEL I AM, WILLIAM HOWE. DO YOU REPENT YOUR SINS...?
YES, SWEET ANGEL. GOD FORGIVE ME, I REPENT THEM ALL...
Thou art all fair, my love; thou hast ravished my heart...
THEN THE KINGDOM OF HEAVEN IS YOURS...

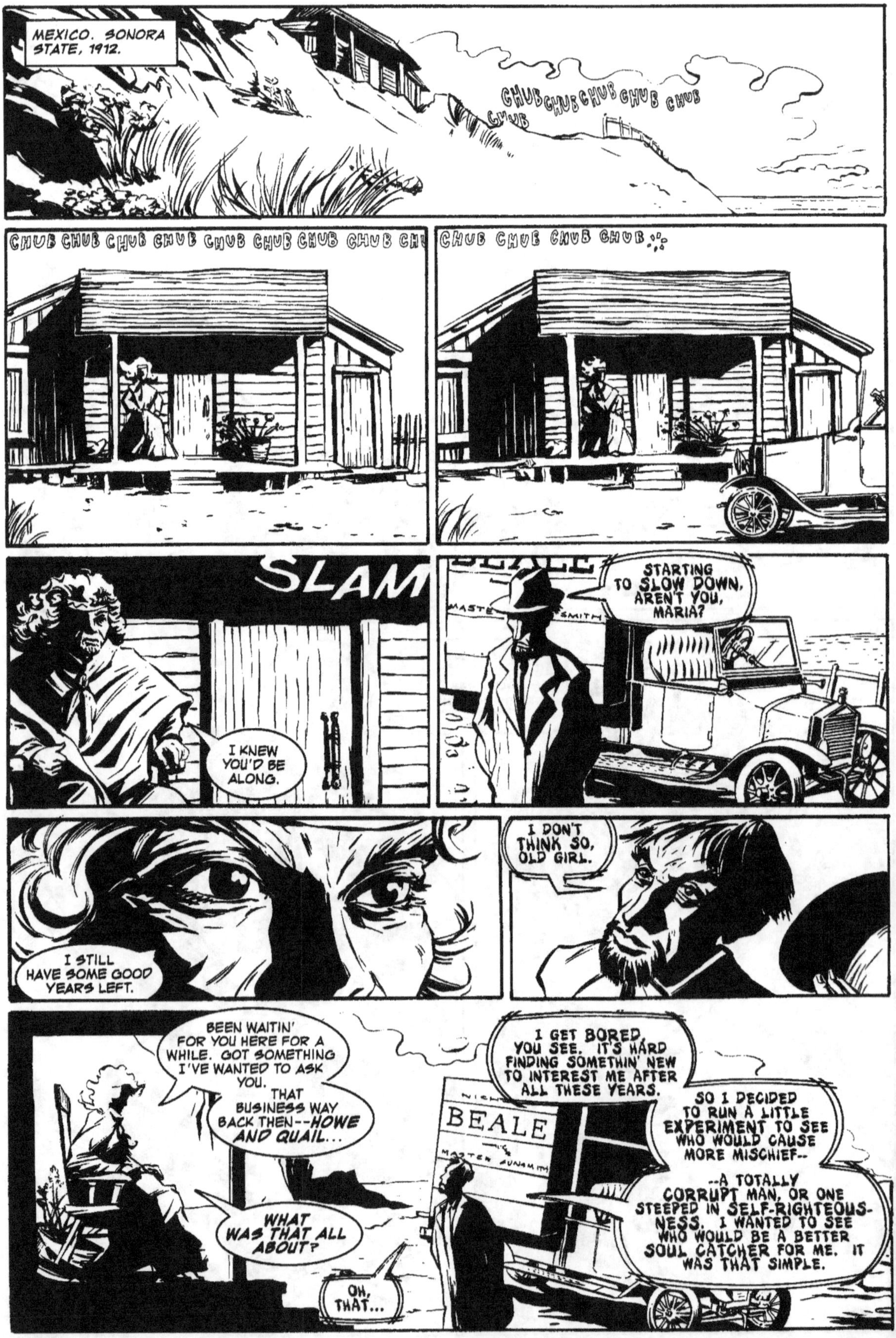

Creating Demon Gun is an intensely personal experience. I've worked closely with Billy Tucci at CRUSADE, learning the ins and outs of self-publishing as we've striven to create the best comics in the industry. Still, these have been Billy's books, the creatures of his imagination far more than mine, and the burden of making them happen ultimately has fallen on his shoulders, not mine, even when I was the editor.

Demon Gun is different, It's my book (and Barry's, of course), and I'm the one sweating out every detail of its creation and production. This has been a firsthand lesson in how excrutiating the process of self-publishing comics can be, and one of the lessons is that every step takes more time than you project, even when you think you're being generous.

Once again, we've put our hearts and souls into the effort, but you the readers are the final arbiters of whether we've succeeded or not.

A number of readers have asked about Howe's unusual guns. In Demon Gun #1, Sheriff Lucas offered a bit of description, noting that they are the customwork of a notorious gunsmith named Beale. Still, I'd like to provide some more detail for those of you interested in such things:

Howe's "long gun" is a Volcanic pistol. The Volcanic Company produced their handguns from about 1855 to 1859, in very limited numbers (an Italian Gunsmith named Venditti produced virtual reproductions of Volcanics for European customers as late as the 1880s, but by then the design was helplessly obsolete). The Volcanic handgun represented the first use of the "lever-action" that was later to become the hugely successful Winchester rifle (initially the Henry rifle). The larger Volcanics such as Howe's carried ten shots. The real design flaw of the Volcanic handgun was it's cartridge, a 36 caliber round with a very weak load of powder, making it a very anemic weapon when compared to such contemporary hand-cannons as the Walker Model Colt .44 revolver.

The Henry and Winchester rifle fixed this problem with a very effective .44 caliber cartridge, and Howe's weapon has been rechambered for this round, at the loss of two shots. Unlike most revolvers of the Civil War era, Howe's special shorty uses self-contained, brass-jacketed cartridges rather than paper cartridges and lead balls, making it a much faster weapon to reload. So, with his two guns, Howe is capable of producing (by 1866 standards) an impressive volume, weight, and rate of fire.

As you can tell, Barry and I have been trying to ensure that the historical details and background detail of Demon Gun are accurate. The lancers in this issue, for example, are part of the French expeditionary force that occupied Mexico from 1861 to early 1867 in the attempt to prop up the ill-fated monarchy of the Emperor Maximilian. A fine account of this little-known period can be found in Jasper Ridley's Maximillian and Juarez (Ticknor and Fields, 1992).

As for the unpleasant Col. Gideon Quail, he is patterned after several famous confederate raiders, and you can read about the history of these fighters (many of whom fled across the Mexico border after Lee's surrender) in The Civil War in the American West, by Alvin M. Josephy, Jr. (Vintage, 1991). If we have in any way sparked your interest in the remarkable events transpiring in the American Southwest during and after the Civil War, prowl your local library or bookstore, and I promise that you'll be fascinated by what you find...although there won't be any supernaturally possessed preachers (that I know of, anyhow)!

Gary Cohn

Parting Shots

Well, friends, our tale is told, our song is sung. All our characters have made their choices and met their fates, and only the Devil is left standing. But he really lost this game, although he'd never admit it. Of course, we don't know what Maria has been up to for the nearly half-century she wore her paired Thunderers... Maybe that's a story for another time.

I hope that those of you who stayed the course with us are satisfied with how DEMON GUN has unfolded. We hit some bumps in the road as far as getting the book out in timely fashion...but we persevered. And now the tale of Preacher Howe wants to be told in other media. I dream of this story as a movie (imagine Harrison Ford, Lance Henrikson or Clint Eastwood as Howe...) A composer friend suggests DEMON GUN: THE OPERA (!) and I really like the idea, so we're starting to discuss how to make that happen. Sometime soon Barry and I may rework this into an interesting trade paperback package, and there might be a colored, CD-Rom version. My modelmaker friends are still interested in producing a DEMON GUN figure... somehow or other there's an afterlife for this tale.

I've really enjoyed creating DEMON GUN, and I know Barry Orkin has as well. The reader response has been truly remarkable, and I thank all of you who took time out to tell us that you were enjoying our work. We promised a special portrait of Howe for all our correspondents, and Barry is working on it--expect yours to show up when you least expect it (but sooner rather than later). As for our Colt replica giveaway, the winner was Rev. Leonard Smith of Springfield, Missouri, and I hope he's happy with the model (let us know, Rev. Smith, okay?). Just this past week I was thrilled to find replicas of the Volcanic handgun in the Smokey Mountain Knifeworks catalog (po Box 4430, Sevierville, TN 37864) and immediately ordered one for me and one for Barry. Check 'em out!

DEMON GUN is a story of redemption through repentance, and the redeeming power of love. Howe progresses from an Old Testament model of faith to a New Testament understanding of his plight, from punishment to forgiveness. His unacknowledged love for Maria, which he resists and denies, forces him to confront who he is and what he's done. Her love is the catalyst for his salvation.

Stories of retribution externalize sin--we imagine that we can purify ourselves by destroying others who we perceive as evil and the sources of our dis-ease--our sense of the world as a demon-haunted place. Howe takes grim satisfaction in his self-righteous pursuit of the men who destroyed his town. But it's a false righteousness, and finally he is forced to confront the darkness within himself. He must accept that external evil is a reflection of his inner self...of all our selves.

Until that happens he cannot be redeemed. He must recognize his own sinfulness, repent, atone through suffering, and embrace forgiveness and lovingkindness. Only then will he find salvation. Otherwise he's locked into a neverending cycle of vengeance--doing the Devil's work. Throughout the story he talks about God, but it's only at the end, when he gains redemption, that he speaks the name of Christ. At last he understands and embraces the true message of the faith he professes, and so he dies in a state of grace.

I've enjoyed the opportunity to explore this religious perspective through these characters, this situation and setting, and I want to express my gratitude to Crusade's William Tucci for giving me the chance to make DEMON GUN a reality. And to all of you who stuck with us for these three issues, my heartfelt thanks. We'll be seeing more of each other.

–GARY COHN

AFTERWORD
DEMON GUN TWENTY YEARS AFTER THE LAST SHOTS...

For years after Crusade published DEMON GUN, Barry Orkin and I considered a future for the tale. David Bernstein of Grand Design, now a good friend of many years, became our agent representing the property. A producer took a small option on it, he and a screenwriter wrote a screenplay that deviated from our story in ways I wasn't entirely happy with. That screenplay, I was told, made the rounds through various studios in Hollywood, never quite catching fire. Eventually life moved on, and DEMON GUN became an artifact of my past.

But I've never been content with that. DEMON GUN is the only thing I've created that I own (with Barry), that has ever been published in wide distribution. It's a story I carried with me for almost twenty years before I ever got to turn it into a comic. That seemed like a long time, but now I know it wasn't all that long. I'm considerably older now than Preacher Howe is in the story, and he still walks with me. There's something not quite finished here. He's found his redemption...but what about Maria?

It's a great pleasure to me that we can now offer this very limited run of the original three- chapter story. I'm very happy to be able to let new readers react as they will to Howe and his struggle. But there needs to be something more. A sequel, perhaps? Barry and I always talked about DEMON GUN 2: AVE MARIA. After all, Maria has forty years of adventures between the moment she picks up the two Volcanics and the day the Devil comes to take them back. So, maybe. But for now, I'm happy to have this small run of new copies, and some of them are going to go to people who might be helpful in giving this story more life.

For you, the reader, I do hope that you've enjoyed this tale. As the three text pieces from the original publication make clear, it was a labor of love, and I put some serious thought and heart into it. The art still stands up, although Barry's NEW work, twenty years later, is far more impressive (find STOKER AND WELLS, written by the great Steven Peros). Still, his talent was obvious even back then. I feel that he made a really good choice in going for a woodblock print effect with this comic. It's a distinctive style that carries the story along very effectively, and his big splash and action scenes are gorgeous. We've talked sometimes about doing a color version, and maybe that will happen someday (although the days grow short), but for now, it was a book designed for the effects of black and white, and it works very well that way.

I was a young man in my mid-twenties when I first thought of Howe, in the mid-1970s. I was a middle-aged man in the mid-1990s when Barry and I brought him to life. I'm on the edge of being an old man now, another twenty years later, as I consider what life I might still give the good preacher. For now, this is your copy of DEMON GUN. I hope it has been a good read for you, and I hope even more that it has given you some food for thought. If you have anything you'd like to say to me about it, my email address is below.

Thanks for taking this ride with us.

—Gary Cohn, March, 2019 wordslingergc@gmail.com

www.ingramcontent.com/pod-product-compliance
Lightning Source LLC
Chambersburg PA
CBHW081145170626
46809CB00011B/3159